NEBRASKA CORNHUSKERS

BY JIM GIGLIOTTI

Published by The Child's World®
1980 Lookout Drive • Mankato, MN 56003-1705
800-599-READ • www.childsworld.com

Copyright ©2022 by The Child's World®
All rights reserved. No part of this book may be reproduced or utilized in any form or by any means without written permission from the publisher.

Cover: Brian Murphy/Icon Sportswire/AP Photo.
Interior: AP Photo: Bob Gorham/Lincoln Journal 8; Dave Weaver 19. Shutterstock: rthoma 4. Newscom: Albert Dickson/Sporting News 11; Bryan Lynn/Icon Sportwire 15; Jeff Tuttle/KRT 16; Keith Gillett/Icon Sportswire 21. Shutterstock: Bob Cullinan 12. Wikimedia: 7 (2).

ISBN 9781503850422 (Reinforced Library Binding)
ISBN 9781503850613 (Portable Document Format)
ISBN 9781503851375 (Online Multi-user eBook)
LCCN: 2021930326

Printed in the United States of America

Wan'Dale Robinson continues a long tradition of Huskers stars.

CONTENTS

Why We Love College Football   4

CHAPTER ONE
Early Days   6

CHAPTER TWO
Glory Years   9

CHAPTER THREE
Best Year Ever!   10

CHAPTER FOUR
Nebraska Traditions   13

CHAPTER FIVE
Meet the Mascot   14

CHAPTER SIX
Top Nebraska QBs   17

CHAPTER SEVEN
Other Nebraska Heroes   18

CHAPTER EIGHT
Recent Superstars   21

Glossary   22
Find Out More   23
Index   24

WHY WE LOVE COLLEGE FOOTBALL

The leaves are changing color. Happy crowds fill the stadiums. Pennants wave. And here come the fight songs. It's time for college football! The sport is one of America's most popular. Millions of fans follow their favorite teams. They wear school colors and hope for big wins.

The University of Nebraska is one of college football's best. Its long history includes lots of championships. Great players have worn the scarlet and cream colors. Let's meet the famous Cornhuskers!

The Cornhuskers play at Memorial Stadium in Lincoln, Nebraska.

CHAPTER ONE

Early Days

Nebraska played its first game in 1890. The team won that game. It won its only other game that season, too. That was a sign of things to come. The team has been a big winner ever since.

The early Huskers became a power in the Midwest. The team won all nine games it played in 1902. The Huskers didn't give up a single point all season! The team went 46-8-1 under Coach Bummy Booth from 1900-05. That was a tough act to follow. But Coach Jumbo Stiehm led the team to a 35-2-3 mark from 1911-15.

> **GO, BUGEATERS!**
> Nebraska was known by several different nicknames in its early years. One of them was the Bugeaters! Coach Bummy Booth changed it to Cornhuskers in 1900. The name is often shortened to Huskers.

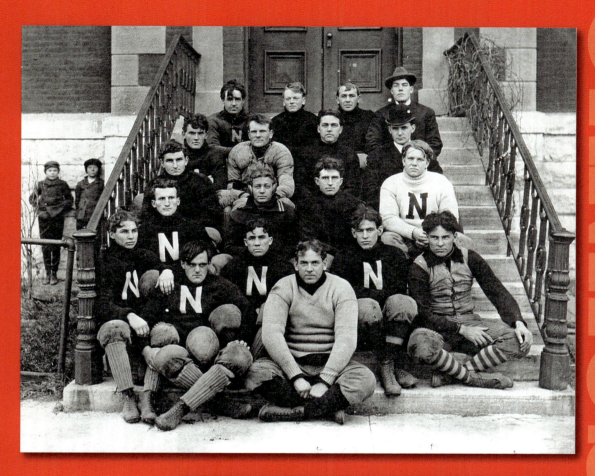

Above: The 1901 Huskers only lost two games.

Right: The 1902 team did even better—they won all 10 games!

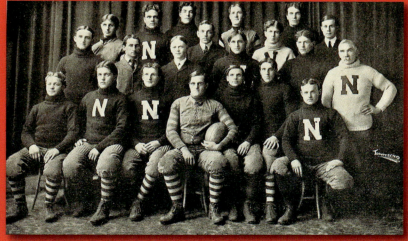

CHAPTER TWO

Glory Years

There have been many stretches of great play in Nebraska football history. The best came from 1993 to 1997. The Huskers played 63 games in those five seasons. They won 60 of them! The 1994 and '95 teams won back-to-back national titles. The 1997 team won another championship.

> **COACH CONGRESSMAN**
> Tom Osborne was the Huskers' head coach for 25 years beginning in 1973. He led the team to 255 wins. Huskers fans loved him! After he stopped coaching, he was elected to the U.S. House of Representatives.

That was the fifth national title for Nebraska. The others came in 1970 and '71. Both those teams were **undefeated**. The 1971 Huskers did something no other team has ever done. No. 1 Nebraska beat the teams that finished No. 2, No. 3, and No. 4 in the final rankings.

Left: Quarterback Scott Frost led Nebraska to its 1997 championship.

CHAPTER THREE

Best Year Ever!

College football celebrated its 150th anniversary in 2019. ESPN ranked the top 150 teams of all-time. Who was No. 1 on the list? The 1971 Nebraska Cornhuskers.

The 1971 team's most famous game was played on Thanksgiving Day. Nebraska faced No. 2 Oklahoma. The Huskers won an exciting game 35–31. The winning touchdown came late in the fourth quarter. It was called the "Game of the **Century**."

Coach Bob Devaney's team **clinched** the national title with a 38–6 **rout** of Alabama in the Orange Bowl.

> **FIESTA TIME!**
>
> The 1995 Huskers were another of college football's greatest teams ever. The team scored at least 35 points in all 13 games. It beat every opponent by at least 14 points. It capped the season by clobbering No. 2 Florida 62–24 in the Fiesta Bowl.

Johnny Rodgers (20) sprints toward the end zone in a big win over Oklahoma in 1971.

CHAPTER FOUR

Nebraska Traditions

Memorial Stadium is packed. The fans yell "Husker!" then "Power!" over and over. Music blares. Everyone watches on the huge scoreboards. Nebraska's players run through a tunnel to the field. It's one of the most exciting traditions in college football.

As they run, they tap a lucky horseshoe. It was found in the dirt when the school built the stadium.

The Huskers reach the end of the tunnel. The team races onto the field! It's game time!

THE BIG RIVAL!

Nebraska moved from the **Big 12** to the **Big Ten** in 2011. There was no room on the schedule to play Oklahoma anymore. The Sooners were the Huskers' long-time **rival**. Now they've found a new one. Nebraska and Iowa play each year for the Heroes Trophy.

← *Left: Former QB Scott Frost became Nebraska's coach in 2018. He leads the team onto the field from the tunnel for each game.*

CHAPTER FIVE

Meet the Mascot

Herbie the Husker is the team's costumed mascot. The husk is the outer layer of a corncob. A cornhusker removes husks. Cornhusker is a nickname for someone from Nebraska.

Herbie wears a red shirt, blue jeans, and work boots. He also has a big, red cowboy hat! Herbie's first game was in the 1973 season. He is now joined on the sidelines by Lil' Red. Lil' Red was created in 1993 to help kids cheer. His costume is **inflatable**. Lil' Red may be almost 30 years old now, but he still has a little kid's personality!

> **SEA OF RED**
>
> The Huskers play their home games at Memorial Stadium. Everyone wears red! The fans cheer their team. They also applaud the other team after every game. It doesn't matter if the Huskers win or lose. It's a great show of **sportsmanship**.

Right: Inside this giant Herbie head, a Nebraska student leads cheers for the great football team.

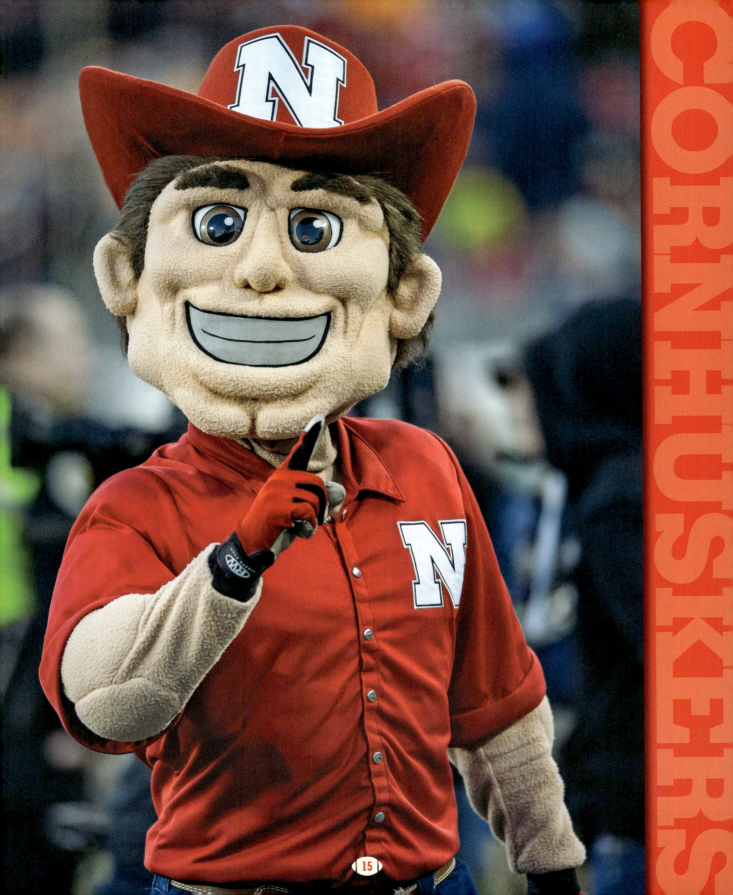

CHAPTER SIX

Top Nebraska QBs

What is a quarterback's No. 1 job? To lead his team to victory! In that case, the Huskers' greatest QB was Tommie Frazier. He guided Nebraska to wins in 33 of his 36 starts. He was the QB for the national title teams of 1994 and '95.

Turner Gill was another big winner at quarterback. The Huskers won 33 of his 38 starts from 1981 to 1983.

In 2001, QB Eric Crouch won the Heisman Trophy. The award is given to college football's top player each year. Crouch was a great runner and passer.

NEBRASKA'S HEISMAN WINNERS
Johnny Rodgers, 1972
Mike Rozier, 1983
Eric Crouch, 2001

— *Left: Tommie Frazier was a great passer, runner, and leader for the Huskers.*

CHAPTER SEVEN

Other Nebraska Heroes

Nebraska has always been known for great **offensive linemen**. Boomer Brown, Will Shields, and Dean Steinkuhler are among them. They helped Huskers' backs run for lots of yards. Mike Rozier gained the most. He ran for 4,780 yards from 1981–83.

RIMINGTON TROPHY
Dave Rimington was a great **center** from 1979–82. The best center in college football now gets the Rimington Trophy. The first winner of the Rimington Trophy also played for the Huskers. That was Dominic Raiola in 2000.

Huskers' defensive players are called the Blackshirts. Trev Alberts was the nation's top linebacker in 1993. In the 2000s, Ndamukong Suh was one of the best Blackshirts. Suh was named college football's best defensive player in 2009.

Right: Look out below! Ndamukong Suh rises up to block a pass.

CHAPTER EIGHT

Recent Superstars

Some recent Huskers have been among the best offensive players in school history. In 2010, Roy Helu Jr. rushed for an amazing 307 yards in a single game against Missouri. That set a school record.

Ameer Abdullah ran for 4,588 yards from 2011–2013. He is second only to Mike Rozier on the school's all-time list in that category.

Tommy Armstrong Jr. passed for a Huskers-record 8,871 yards from 2013–16. Receiver Stanley Morgan Jr. set another school record. He had 189 catches from 2014–18.

But look out, Stanley! Wan'Dale Robinson is quickly moving up the charts. He entered 2021 with 91 catches in only 18 career games.

Who will be the next Nebraska superstar?

Left: Wan'Dale Robinson heads to the end zone for another Nebraska TD.

GLOSSARY

Big 12 (BIG TWELVE) the name of the conference, or group of teams, in which the Huskers played from 1996–2010

Big Ten (BIG TEN) the name of the conference, or group of teams, in which the Huskers now play

center (SEN-ter) a position on the offensive line that snaps the ball to the quarterback

century (SEN-chur-ee) a period of 100 years

clinched (KLINCHT) achieved for certain

inflatable (in-FLAYT-uh-bull) filled with air

offensive linemen (AW-fen-siv LYNE-men) players who block for the quarterback and runners

rival (RYE-vul) an individual or team that competes for the same thing

rout (ROWT) a victory by a lot of points

sportsmanship (SPORTS-men-ship) fair play and nice behavior in competition

undefeated (un-deh-FEE-ted) not losing any games

FIND OUT MORE

IN THE LIBRARY

Jacobs, Greg. *The Everything Kids' Football Book*. New York: Adams Media, 2015.

Sports Illustrated for Kids. *The Greatest Football Teams of All Time*. New York: Sports Illustrated Kids, 2018.

Weber, Margaret. *Nebraska Cornhuskers*. New York: Weigl, 2019.

ON THE WEB

Visit our website for links about the
Nebraska Cornhuskers:
childsworld.com/links

Note to Parents, Teachers, and Librarians: We routinely verify our Web links to make sure they are safe and active sites. So encourage your readers to check them out!

INDEX

Abdullah, Ameer 21
Alabama 10
Alberts, Trev 18
Armstrong, Tommy Jr. 21
Blackshirts 18
Booth, Bummy 6
Brown, Boomer 18
Bugeaters 6
Crouch, Eric 17
Devaney, Bob, 10
ESPN 10
Fiesta Bowl 10
Florida State 10
Frazier, Tommie 17
Frost, Scott 9, 13
Gill, Turner 17
Helu, Roy Jr. 21
Herbie the Husker 14
Iowa 13
Memorial Stadium 5, 13, 14
Morgan, Stanley Jr. 21
Oklahoma 10, 11, 13
Osborne, Tom 9
Raiola, Dominic 18
Rimington, Dean 18
Robinson, Wan'Dale 2, 21
Rodgers, Johnny 11, 17
Rozier, Mike 17, 18, 21
Shields, Will 18
Steinkuhler, Dean 18
Stiehm, Jumbo 6
Suh, Ndamukong 18

ABOUT THE AUTHOR

Jim Gigliotti has written more than 100 books for young readers, many of them on sports. He attended the University of Southern California and worked in the athletic department for the Trojans—another of college football's best teams!